I Took My Frog to the Library

I Took My Frog
to the Library

Eric A. Kimmel

Pictures by
Blanche Sims

PUFFIN BOOKS

PUFFIN BOOKS

Published by the Penguin Group

Penguin Putnam Books for Young Readers, 345 Hudson Street,
New York, New York 10014, U.S.A.

Penguin Books Ltd, 27 Wrights Lane, London W8 5TZ, England

Penguin Books Australia Ltd, Ringwood, Victoria, Australia

Penguin Books Canada Ltd, 10 Alcorn Avenue, Toronto, Ontario, Canada M4V 3B2

Penguin Books (N.Z.) Ltd, 182-190 Wairau Road, Auckland 10, New Zealand

Penguin Books Ltd, Registered Offices: Harmondsworth, Middlesex, England

First published in the United States of America by Viking Penguin,
a division of Penguin Books USA Inc. 1990
Published in Puffin Books, 1992

17   19   20   18   16

Text copyright © Eric A. Kimmel, 1990
Illustrations copyright © Blanche Sims, 1990
LIBRARY OF CONGRESS CATALOGING-IN-PUBLICATION DATA

Kimmel, Eric A.

I took my frog to the library / by Eric A. Kimmel ; illustrated by
Blanche Sims.   p.   cm.

"First published in the United States of America by Viking Penguin
. . . 1990"—T.p. verso.

Summary: A young girl brings her pets to the library—with
predictably disastrous results.

ISBN 0-14-050916-X (pbk.)

[1. Pets—Fiction. 2. Libraries—Fiction.]   I. Sims, Blanche.
ill.   II. Title.

[PZ7.K5648Iat   1992]   [E]—dc20   91-30164

Printed in the United States of America

Set in Century Expanded

To Bridgett
E.A.K.

I took my frog to the library,

but he jumped on the checkout desk

and scared the librarian.

I took my hen to the library,

but she laid an egg in the card catalog.

I took my pelican to the library,
but he hid the dictionary in his pouch
and no one could find it.

I took my python to the library,

but she shed her skin all over the picture books.

I took my giraffe to the library,
but he tried to read over everybody's shoulder.

I took my hyena to the library,
but he laughed so loud during storytime
that nobody could hear the story.

I took my elephant to the library.

My elephant is very well behaved.

She stacked her books neatly on the checkout desk.

She asked the librarian's help when she needed it.

She listened to the story and laughed in all

the right places.

But my elephant is very big.

So big!

So big!!

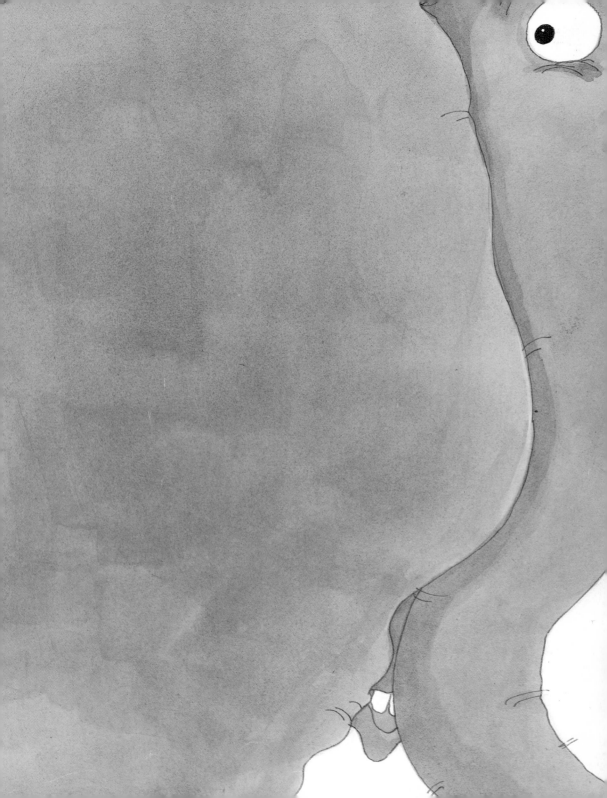

SO BIG!!!

She wrecked the library.

The librarian said, "Bridgett, you are always welcome in the library. But the next time you come to the library,

please leave your animals at home."

LA LA LA

So, whenever I go to the library,
my frog stays home,
my hen stays home,
my pelican stays home,
my python stays home,
my giraffe stays home,
my hyena stays home,